UNCLE LEO'S ADVENTURES
in the
Swiss Desert

Yannets Levi has written books and for television. Born in Israel to a family of storytellers, he remembers being surrounded by stories ever since he was a kid, told by his parents, uncles and aunts.

His Uncle Leo's Adventures series is one of Israel's most popular children's book series and has sold more than 450,000 copies in Israel alone. The series has also been published in the Czech Republic, South Korea and Japan. He has also written another children's book, *Mrs Rosebud is No Monster,* and two books for adults.

Yaniv Shimony is a graduate of the Bezalel Academy of Art and Design in Jerusalem, considered the top art school in Israel. After completing his studies, he worked as Art Director in some of Israel's largest advertising agencies. Currently, his work focuses on illustrating children's books. In 2008, Shimony won an award for Children's Book Illustration from the Israel Museum for his work in *Uncle Leo's Adventures in the Romanian Steppes.*

Other Books in the Series:

UNCLE LEO'S
ADVENTURES
in the
SWISS DESERT

Yannets Levi

Illustrated by Yaniv Shimony
Translated by Margo Eyon

RED TURTLE
RUPA

For my beloved inbal
—Yannets
For Avishag and Maya
—Yaniv

Published in Red Turtle by
Rupa Publications India Pvt. Ltd 2014
7/16, Ansari Road, Daryaganj
New Delhi 110002

Sales centres:
Allahabad Bengaluru Chennai
Hyderabad Jaipur Kathmandu
Kolkata Mumbai

First published in Hebrew in 2010
This edition copyright © Yannets Levi 2014
Illustration copyright © Yaniv Shimony 2010
Translated by Margo Eyon

This edition published by arrangement with Asia Publishers Int.,
Israel (asia01@netvision.net.il) through Writer's Side, India

ISBN: 978-81-291-3465-3

Second impression 2018

10 9 8 7 6 5 4 3 2

The moral right of the author has been asserted.

This edition is for sale in the Indian subcontinent only.

Printed at Replika Press Pvt. Ltd, India.

Contents

Introduction

If you asked me, I would set new rules for the world. First of all, grown-ups wouldn't get to tell kids what to do. Because when you think about it, what's the difference between children and adults? How would Mom and Dad feel if some big lady were to suddenly barge into their house and say, 'You've had enough chocolate! You've watched enough TV! And it's about time you straightened up your room!' Or if someone told them, 'Stop fighting over nothing!' Because sometimes Mom and Dad fight too, even though they say they're just having a discussion.

But no one tells grown-ups how much chocolate to eat or how long to watch television, or orders them to stop fighting and share their toys. And it's not fair.

I said so to Uncle Leo, and he told me that adults

are children too.

'What do you mean?' I asked.

'Adults are children in the shape of grown-ups,' he explained, and if Uncle Leo says so, it must be true, because Uncle Leo has had crazy adventures all over the world and knows lots of stuff. 'But in the end,' said Uncle Leo, 'it's good that there are children-shaped children and adult-shaped children.'

Uncle Leo comes to visit us every Wednesday. Uncle Leo isn't like any ordinary uncle. My father once said, 'Uncle Leo isn't just any old uncle; he's been internationally patented!'

On Wednesdays, when Uncle Leo comes over, he tells me and my brother about all his adventures in the Swiss desert. And now I'm going to tell them to you. I swear that everything I tell you is true. I didn't make any of it up. I heard it all with my own ears, straight from my Uncle Leo.

And by the way, if you don't know, my name is Andy, my brother's is Graham, and my new baby sister's is Phoebe. My father's name is Eliot, my mother's is Daphne and my Uncle Leo's—as you might have guessed—is Uncle Leo.

Uncle Leo, Superstar

Yesterday we were sitting in the living room when Graham grabbed the remote control and switched channels while I was watching TV. That really bugged me, so I called for Mom.

She came into the living room and whispered, 'Keep it down in here!'

'It's not fair,' I said. 'Graham changed the channel on me.'

'Why do we always have to watch what he wants?' asked Graham.

'"Who Wants to Be Famous?" is on, and I want to see it!'

'First of all, stop shouting. Your sister is sleeping,' said Mom. Phoebe has been sleeping a lot ever since she was born, and Mom always wants us to be quiet. 'And besides, I think it's about time you turned the television off.'

'What!' Graham and I were both shocked.

'Why?' I cried.

'Shhh! You can't sit in front of that screen all day,' Mom answered.

'It's not fair,' I said. 'We haven't seen anything that *I* picked!'

But Mom took the remote and turned the TV off. 'Go do something else,' she said as she walked out of the room. 'Maybe play a game.'

Graham and I were left sitting on the couch.

'It's all your fault!' Graham hissed. 'Now neither of us can watch "Who Wants to Be Famous?". Why did you have to call Mom?'

I had no answer to Graham's question, so I hissed back, 'Why did you change the channel in the middle of my show?'

Graham kept his mouth shut. I guess he didn't have an answer for me, either. We were both silent for a bit, then Graham said to me quietly, 'When I'm older, I'm going to be famous.'

'What are you going to do?' I asked.

'I'm going to be famous, and everyone will know who I am.'

'Okay, but what will you be famous for?'

'What does it matter? The important thing is to be famous,' said Graham.

Right then, Uncle Leo walked into the room.

'Uncle Leo,' I asked quietly. 'Are you famous?'

'What are you talking about?' exclaimed Graham. 'Famous people are on TV and in the newspapers. Uncle Leo isn't in either of those.'

'It's true, I'm not on television or in the newspapers, but I used to be famous,' said Uncle Leo.

'Really?' asked Graham. 'When?'

'When I was in Nullistan,' said Uncle Leo.

'Nulli—what?' I asked.

'Nullistan,' said Uncle Leo.

'What's that? Where is it?' asked Graham.

Uncle Leo sat down and said, 'Nullistan is a country pretty far away from here. It lies in the heart of the Swiss desert. Not only was I famous in Nullistan, I was a superstar.'

'How did you become a superstar?' asked Graham, so Uncle Leo started telling us his story:

'I reached Nullistan during one of my trips through the Swiss desert. The country was covered in posters about an annual contest that was about to take place. The contest had been running for thirty years, but no one had ever won. To win, contestants had to touch their nose with their tongue. The person who succeeded would be treated like royalty and receive amazing prizes. I immediately tried to reach my nose with my tongue and I did it!

"All right!" I cried. "I must take part in this contest, because I can touch my nose with my tongue. I'm going to win honours and prizes!"'

Graham tried to touch his nose with his tongue, but he couldn't do it. I also stuck my tongue out, but no matter how hard I tried, I couldn't get it to reach my nose.

'Can you really do it?' asked Graham.

Uncle Leo instantly stuck out his tongue and touched his nose. Then he continued: 'The contest took place the following day in a giant stadium with a stage at the centre. Masses of people sat in the bleachers and enthusiastically cheered on the contestants. One by one, the competitors got up on stage—children, women, men. All of them tried to reach their noses with their tongues. Some of the people pulled their tongues with their fingers. Others pulled their tongues up with clothes pegs. Still others actually tried pushing their noses down towards their tongues. But no one succeeded in making them touch. One by one, the participants got off the stage in disappointment. Some even cried.

'Finally, my name was called. I was invited to the stage to try and perform the feat. I went up. Since the people in the crowd didn't know me, they fell silent. I stuck out my tongue and, of course, managed to reach my nose. The crowd was quiet for a moment—out of amazement—and then they started cheering with loud cries and wild applause.

'The prime minister and his wife came on stage. The prime minister laid a wreath of flowers around my neck. He turned to the audience and said, "This man, whose name is Uncle Leo, is the first person ever to win the tongue competition. Let's hear it for Uncle Leo! Hip hip hurray! Hip hip hurray! Hip hip hurray!"

'The crowd shouted with more excitement than I had ever heard in my life—"Hurray for Uncle Leo! Hurray! Hurray! Hurray!"

'Servants carried me in a palanquin to a fancy room that had been prepared especially for me. "And in this room we will tend to your every need," said three servants at the doorway.

'I went into the room and lay down on the large bed in the middle of the room. The sheets were luxurious, the pillows were soft, the blanket was warm, and I was tired from my exciting day. I quickly fell asleep. I didn't know that a big surprise was waiting for me the next morning.'

'What happened in the morning?' I asked Uncle Leo.

'I woke up in the morning to the sound of voices singing. I opened my eyes and realized that the voices were coming from the street. I opened the blinds, peeked outside, and was amazed—throngs of people were standing outside around a giant statue.'

Uncle Leo stopped talking now, and his face looked surprised.

'What kind of a statue was it?' asked Graham.

'It was a statue of *me*,' said Uncle Leo. 'Overnight they had made an enormous statue that looked just like me. People were dancing around the statue and singing a one-line song that they kept repeating over and over:

Uncle Leo's like a king! He can do most anything!
Uncle Leo's like a king! He can do most anything!

'I didn't know what to say or do. I was touched and thrilled. I had never seen a statue of me before. I was happy that so many people were singing a song written especially for me. I realized that a lot of people loved me. I hadn't expected the Nullistanis to get so excited about my winning the contest.

'I left the room. The three servants were waiting for me outside the door and accompanied me everywhere. People on the street stopped to stare at me. Painters waited at street corners and tried to draw me really fast. They painted me while I was eating, while I was walking, while I was sitting, when I laughed and when I talked. They drew pictures of everything I did. The pictures were published in the newspapers.

'In this way, the days passed and I quickly became the most famous person in Nullistan. People wanted to look like me. Children, women and men started having their hair done like mine.'

'But how, Uncle Leo? You only have four hairs on your head,' I said.

'Exactly,' said Uncle Leo. 'People asked their barbers to shave their heads, leave only four hairs, and dye them yellow or purple—just like me. But they didn't just copy my hairstyle. Men, women and children started wearing round eyeglasses like mine. Thin people put pillows under their shirts so they could have a pot belly like mine. And it didn't stop there! On one of my visits to the market, I saw lollipops in my likeness for sale. Children walked down the street licking lollipops that looked exactly like me. People on the street wanted to shake my hand and asked me to autograph pictures of myself for them.

'Every day, I ate lunch at the prime minister's residence. Different people were invited to every meal. The prime minister and his wife were of no interest to the guests, who only wanted to meet me. We would talk, and the next day I would read in the newspaper things that I had said:

'My first weeks in Nullistan passed very happily. But as time went by, things got harder for me.'

'What was hard about it?' Graham asked. 'Wasn't it fun?'

'Not really. After a few weeks, it wasn't enjoyable at all. Hordes of people followed me everywhere I went. I couldn't be alone, not even for a moment. The swift painters never stopped drawing everything I did. They even painted me while I took a shower! I wanted privacy. Everyone around me looked the same—exactly like me! Four hairs on their heads, round glasses and a pot belly. I wanted to see people who *didn't* look like me. Almost everything I said appeared in the newspapers. I had to think about every word that came out of my mouth.

'One day, I even saw my face on the new banknotes of Nullistan. That night, in my fancy room, I couldn't fall asleep. I thought, *I don't want to be famous. I don't want everyone to be excited about me like this. I want to be alone. I want to be a regular person. I want to live my life like I used to!* I decided to leave the country right away.

'Very quietly, I tiptoed out of my room. The three servants were asleep on the bench outside the door. If I could get outside without waking them, I could be on my way. But I had only taken one step before one of the servants woke up.

"'Hey!" he said, alarmed. "What's this? What's going on here? Illustrious Uncle Leo, where are you going without us?"

"'Me? I'm not Uncle Leo," I said.

"'But you have glasses and suspenders, just like Uncle Leo," he said.

"'I dress like Uncle Leo because I admire him," I said. "But I'm not Uncle Leo. It's okay, you can go back to sleep."

'The first servant went back to sleep and I started to leave again, but then the second servant woke up.

"'Hey!" he cried. "Where are you going, admirable Uncle Leo?"

"'Me?" I said. "I'm not Uncle Leo. You're mistaken."

"'But you have four hairs on your head, just like Uncle Leo," said the second servant.

"'Well, I like Uncle Leo very much, so I get my hair done like his," I said. "It's okay, you can go back to sleep."

'The second servant also went back to sleep. I just had to get past one more servant. If he didn't wake up, I could get away from there and slip out of Nullistan. But after I had taken just one more step, the third servant awoke.

"'Wait a second! Where are you going, famous Uncle Leo?"

"'Me? I'm not Uncle Leo," I told him.

"'But you have a round belly, just like Uncle Leo," said the third servant.

"'I put a pillow under my shirt so that I can have a pot belly like his, since I'm a big fan of his. But I'm not him," I said.

"'Hold on a minute!" said the servant. "I just want to check." He went into my room and immediately returned.

"'The room is empty. Uncle Leo isn't there. So you *are* Uncle Leo!" called the servant, waking up the other two. All three of them cried, "Renowned Uncle Leo, it *is* you! Where are you going without us? We can't let you go by yourself! Do you need anything? Are you thirsty? Are you hungry? Would you like a glass of milk? Shall we sing you a lullaby?"

"'No," I said disappointedly. "I don't need anything."

I went back to my room. Now I understood that it would not be easy for me to leave Nullistan. For the rest of the night, I tried to think of a solution, and in the morning, I finally had an idea. I decided to ask the prime minister to let me leave the country.

'I went to the prime minister's residence. No sooner had he and his wife seen me than they said, "Uncle Leo, our dear celebrity, we've decided to appoint you minister of Health, Education, Finance and Tourism."

"'But Mr Prime Minister," I said, "I cannot be a government minister! I don't know anything about those things!"

"'Don't know anything? Be serious!" laughed the prime minister and his wife. And then the prime minister said, "Uncle Leo, our wonderful star! We have been holding the tongue contest for thirty years and you are the first person who has been able to complete the task. You're special. You're important to us. You're famous. The citizens of Nullistan love you very much. You'll make a marvellous minister!"

"'Wait a minute, sir and madam," I said to the prime minister and his wife. "Please listen to me. I have a request."

"'Anything you want," said the prime minister.

'I took a deep breath and said, "My dear Mr and Mrs Prime Minister, I would like…I would like…I would like to leave Nullistan."

"'What! Leave our country?'" The prime minister was astonished.

"'Leave *us*?'" cried the prime minister's wife.

"'Um…yes, Mr and Mrs Prime Minister. I would like to leave the country.'"

"'But why? Why leave? You are the most important person in our country. You are the most famous person. All the citizens love you with all their hearts!'"

"'Yes, I know,'" I said. "'That's the problem.'"

"'You don't like it that people love you?'" asked the prime minister's wife, surprised.

"'I like that they love me,'" I told her, "'but I want to be free. I want to continue travelling in the Swiss desert. I want to be alone. I want peace and quiet. I don't want everyone around me to dress like me and get their hair done like mine,'" I explained.

'The prime minister sat down and started to cry. His wife sat down next to him and patted his head.

"'But what will we do without you?'" she asked.

"'What will we do without our Uncle Leo?'" whined the prime minister.

"'Please listen,'" I said. "'I have an idea.'"

"'Whatever you say,'" said the prime minister's wife.

'"Maybe we should hold a new tongue contest," I suggested. "In this contest, the winner will be the person who manages to touch their tongue to their...to their... to their elbow! And that person will be Nullistan's new star!"

'The prime minister and his wife thought for a moment about my suggestion, and then said, "Famous Uncle Leo, we knew we could count on you! That's exactly what we'll do! We have to reinvent ourselves! We must keep up with the times! We shall announce a new contest!"

'That same day, the prime minister announced a new tongue contest. A stage was set up in the middle of the big stadium, and crowds of people came to watch. One by one, contestants got on stage and tried touching their elbows with their tongues. One after another, they failed. I was afraid that no one in Nullistan would be able to do it, but then a little girl went up on the stage and she did it—she touched her elbow with her tongue. The crowd cheered with loud hurrahs and applause. The prime minister's wife put a wreath of flowers around her neck. The prime minister proclaimed her the winner. In a grand procession, the girl was carried in a palanquin to the fancy room.

'I stood on one side. No one paid me any attention. Even when people did see me, they weren't the least bit excited. It seemed like no one even recognized me. No painter tried to paint my picture. No servant tried to serve me. No one asked me for my autograph. Everyone was excited about the little girl who had won the new contest. Everyone had forgotten about me. I left the country and went on my way,' Uncle Leo finished his story.

'And were you sad?' asked Graham.

'I wasn't sad in the end, Graham. After all, if I had continued being the star of Nullistan, I wouldn't have come back from the Swiss desert and I wouldn't have been able to tell you about my adventures.'

That evening, Graham came into the kitchen wearing sunglasses. 'Let's hear it for Graham, the superstar!' he cried.

'Superstar?' asked Mom.

'He wants to be famous,' I explained. 'Like Uncle Leo.'

'Uncle Leo?' Dad said. 'Famous?'

'He was famous in Nullistan,' I said. 'That's a country in the Swiss desert.'

'I'm going to be a singer!' announced Graham.

'A singer!' said Dad. 'Excellent! Did you know that I sang in the choir in first grade? I could have been a great singer!' He started to sing, '*To dream, the impossible dream…*'

Dad sang horribly off-key, but I didn't say anything.

'You could start a band together,' suggested Mom.

'I'll be the drummer!' I said.

'No way!' shouted Graham. 'I'm the drummer!'

'But you're the singer,' I said.

'It's my band,' said Graham. 'I get to say what everyone will be. Mom, are you going to be in the band too?'

'Only if you two get along,' said Mom. 'I don't want to be in a band where there's fighting all the time.'

Graham was quiet for a minute and then said to me, 'All right, you can be the drummer.'

'Wonderful,' said Mom. 'And Phoebe and I will be the audience. Every band needs someone in the audience, right?'

'But wait, will I get to sing too?' asked Dad.

'Only if you don't fight with anyone,' I told him.

Uncle Leo and the
Miraculous Medicine

When I woke up the next morning, I had a sore throat. I didn't feel well. I felt sick. Mom checked my forehead.

'You have a fever,' she said. 'You're staying home today.'

Of course, being sick is no fun. But there's one good thing about it: staying home.

When I stay home sick, Mom lets me watch as much TV as I want. I lie on the couch under a blanket, and Mom or Dad makes all my favourite foods and lets me eat in the living room. So when Mom said I was staying home, I smiled a little even though I didn't feel too good. Graham gave me a dirty look. He had to go to school.

But after Graham had left for school and I was lying on the couch in the living room, I was disappointed. I was disappointed because I found out the TV wasn't working, and I couldn't watch any of my shows. And I was disappointed because Mom was busy all the time with my little sister Phoebe. She didn't give me any special treatment at all. I just lay there on the couch, all by myself. I started to miss my brother Graham. I knew that if he were in the living room now we would probably be fighting, but I missed him anyway.

I lay on the couch and remembered that being sick isn't actually any fun. But then Mom came in and said, 'I ordered a special service for you, a storytelling service.'

'A storytelling service?' I said. I didn't understand what she meant until Uncle Leo walked into the living room. He sat down on the couch next to me, and Mom went to take care of Phoebe.

'Andy,' said Uncle Leo with a sad look. 'I have to tell you that I did something wrong. *Very* wrong.'

'What did you do?' I asked.

'I'm really sorry, Andy. If I hadn't done it, you wouldn't

be sick,' said Uncle Leo.

'What do you mean? What does my being sick have to do with you?' I asked.

'If I had done what needed to be done, no one in the world would have ever been sick again,' said Uncle Leo.

I gave Uncle Leo a questioning look, and he said, 'I'll tell you about it. Once, while I was travelling in the Swiss desert, I came upon a big house. It was late at night, and I didn't know where I would be sleeping, so I decided to ask if the people living there could put me up for the night. I went to the door and knocked, but then I realized that the door was already open. "Hello!" I called out. "Is anybody home?"

'No one answered. The house was empty. I went inside and saw a large room. A fire was burning in the fireplace. I went through the house, from room to room, but everything was silent. No one appeared. Everything was in its proper place, but there were no people around.

'A table stood in the corner of the large room, and on it was a chunk of Swiss cheese, a loaf of bread, and some bowls of hot soup. In the middle of the table was an old book with an interesting title:

'"*The Secret of Medicine?*" I wondered alond. I picked up the book, started reading it, and discovered that this was no regular book; this was a very special book.'

'What was so special about the book?' I asked.

'It said at the beginning that this was an enchanted book. It said that the book appeared once every 2,563 years and then disappeared. I kept reading and soon realized that the book explained how to get hold of a medicine that would cure *every* disease in the world!'

'Every disease?'

'Every last one of them,' said Uncle Leo. 'Anyone who drank the medicine would immediately recover and never get sick again, ever. The medicine would never run out either, so there would be enough for everyone.'

'All diseases would be gone?' I asked. 'Sore throats, too?'

'Yes,' answered Uncle Leo. 'Sore throats too.'

'The flu? Fevers? Stomach aches?'

'Yes.'

'Even scrapes?'

'Even scrapes,' said Uncle Leo. 'Every illness, every pain, every ache would be gone if anyone drank the medicine. I knew that if I just followed the instructions in the book, I would be able to get hold of the medicine, and no boy or girl, no man or woman, would ever be sick again in their whole lives!

'The book explained that the medicine was located in a silver flask in a dark cave. The entrance to the cave was hidden behind a door in the floor beneath the table. I bent down, found the door, opened it, and saw that there really was a cave under there. I checked the book for the next instruction, and found this warning:

if
you want to
reach the
medicine,
Don't eat or
drink in the cave.

'"Don't eat or drink? That's no problem," I said to myself and immediately decided to enter the cave, find the magic medicine, and save the world from all illnesses. But when I entered the cave, I couldn't believe my eyes!'

Uncle Leo stopped talking. He closed his eyes, and sniffed so hard that his nostrils flared.

'Uncle Leo, what did you see in the cave?' I asked.

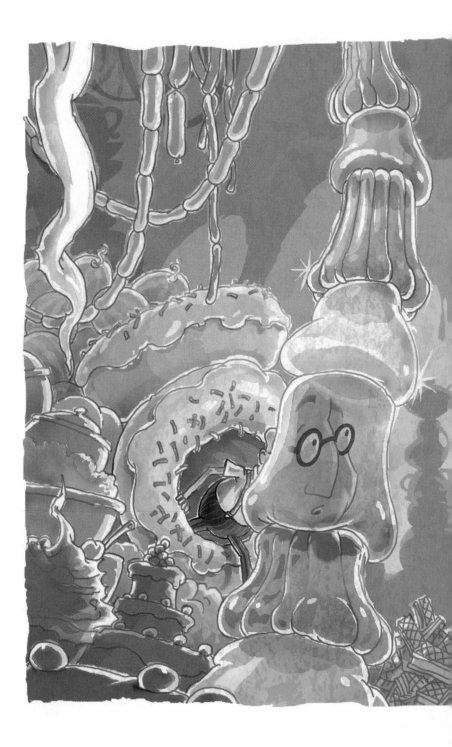

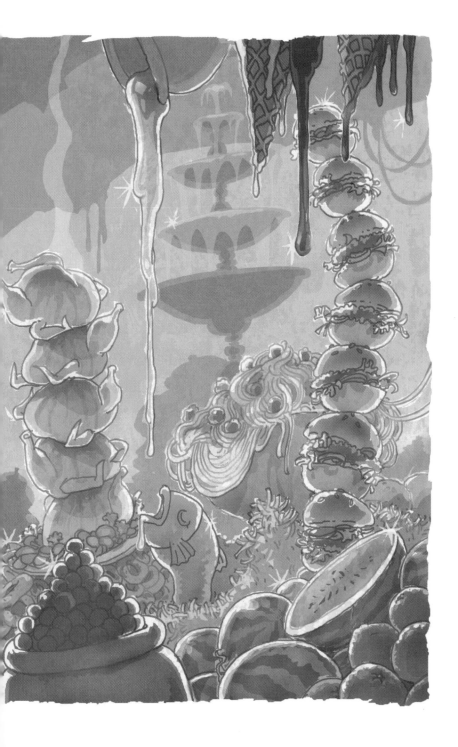

'I saw food in the cave. I saw all the tastiest foods in the world! There were shelves and tables loaded with cream cakes, fresh fruit, cooked delicacies, and juices in every flavour.'

'Was there spaghetti too?' I asked.

'Andy, there was pasta in every shape and size, and with every kind of sauce. Every type of mouth-watering food that you can imagine was in the cave. And all of it looked so delicious and tempting! But I remembered that if I wanted to reach the medicine that would cure all the illnesses in the world, I was forbidden from eating anything as long as I was in the cave. So I didn't touch the food. I kept on going. The cave went deeper and deeper, and the marvellous smells from the food all around nearly drove me out of my mind.

'I followed the instructions in the book until I reached a tiny door. The book said that the flask containing the medicine was behind that door. I went up to the door, but it didn't have a handle or a lock, and I didn't know how to open it. I looked in the book, searching for an answer. I flipped through the pages until I found written on one of them:

When you reach
the door,
command it to
open.

'I looked at the door and said in my most commanding voice, "Open immediately, door!"

'"What? What kind of attitude is that?" said a voice. At first I was surprised, but then I understood that the door was talking to me.

'"What do I look like to you?" the door snapped. "Is that how you should talk to me? If you want something, ask nicely. I'm nobody's servant in this cave! I want you to leave, come back and then ask me in a civilized manner," yelled the door.

'I didn't want to quarrel with the door. I wanted to get to the medicine that was behind it. So I moved away, then came back and said in a gentle voice, "Excuse me, most honourable door, please pardon the intrusion, but perhaps you could be so kind as to open up?"

"'That's more like it, that's how it should be. Now, was that so hard?" said the door in a pleased voice, and opened.

'Behind the door there was a small silver flask. I knew that inside that flask was the magic medicine. I was very happy. I picked up the flask, looked in the book, followed the path, and started making my way out of the cave.'

'Uncle Leo,' I said, 'maybe I could drink some of that medicine?'

'I wish you could!' said Uncle Leo. 'I only wish,' he added, and continued with his story. 'The way out of the cave was much longer than the way in. It went on for two days, maybe longer. I didn't know if the sun was rising or setting outside. I walked on and on, and got very tired and hungry. This time, when I passed the shelves and tables full of delicacies, I had to struggle to keep from tasting anything. It wasn't easy. There were incredible dishes all around: strawberry cakes with whipped cream, noodles, ice cream, rice, all kinds of juices, seasoned potatoes, crunchy cookies, quiches, candy of every size and color—all the best foods in the world. I was so hungry, my stomach was rumbling. My mouth ached to taste the food. But I told myself, "I won't taste anything. I'm going on."

'A long time passed before I saw the light at the end of the cave. "There, in just another minute, I'll be out of here and then I can eat something and also save the world from all disease," I kept saying to myself. I walked until I had almost reached the cave's exit.

'Right next to the exit was a little table. On the table there was a tray and on the tray there was a tall tower of Swiss cheese cubes. I looked at the cheese and felt my mouth salivate. I felt my stomach begging me to take a bite. I felt my hands itching to touch the cheese cubes. Just one crumb, just a crumblet, just a tidbit of a crumblet. "I'll be outside in a second," I told myself. "I'm right next to the exit out of the cave. What difference would it make now? I'll just have the tiniest taste of this wonderful cheese. Just a smidgeony-smidgeon. It won't count."

'I stretched out my hand and broke off a teensy-weensy crumb from one of the cubes. I smelled it. The smell was so tempting. I put the crumblet in my mouth. Even though the crumblet was so tiny, it tasted delicious. "There we go, everything's fine," I said to myself. "Nothing happened. Now I'll just leave the cave and save the world from all disease!"

'I continued on. I thought I would be outside the cave any second, but though I walked and walked and walked, I didn't reach the exit. It seemed like it was just getting further away from me. I felt myself getting more and more tired. I felt like I was standing in one place. I looked down at my feet and was shocked.'

Uncle Leo now shook his head from side to side and looked at me with terrible fear in his eyes.

'What happened, Uncle Leo? What happened to your feet?' I asked.

'My feet? They had turned into Swiss cheese! At first just my toes, then my feet, then my calves, then my thighs and then my stomach. I knew that pretty soon my whole

body would turn into Swiss cheese, and I—I would simply become a block of Swiss cheese and stay forever in the cave. "What strange illness has set upon me?" I cried. "Those cheese cubes were bewitched! Why did I eat in the cave?" I didn't know what to do. But then I remembered that I was holding the flask with the miraculous medicine. The medicine could cure any disease in the world! It would save me from this strange disease. I didn't hesitate—my chest had already turned into Swiss cheese! I opened the flask and took a sip of the medicine. Just in the nick of time. No sooner had I drunk it than the medicine immediately disappeared, along with the cave and the enchanted book. The big empty house also vanished. I found myself standing alone in a field. I looked at my body and saw that it had gone back to being human. The medicine had cured me. I was saved.

'I knew that the book would reappear only in another 2,563 years. I looked around and saw a block of Swiss cheese at my feet. I sat down on a rock in the field and ate the cheese. After all, I was still very hungry,' Uncle Leo concluded his story.

'It's too bad you didn't manage to get the medicine out of the cave,' I said. 'But it's a good thing that you saved your life.'

'Yes,' said Uncle Leo. 'Everything has its advantages and disadvantages.'

At dinner that night, Graham said, 'Mom, I don't feel well, either.'

Mom looked down his throat, placed a hand on his forehead, and said, 'You might have a fever.'

'So neither of us will go to school tomorrow?' Graham asked.

'Possibly,' said Mom.

'And we can watch TV and eat in the living room?' Graham asked.

'Yes,' said Mom. 'The television has been fixed.'

Dad looked at us. He put his hand on his own forehead and asked Mom, 'Could you check my throat, too?'

Mom peered down Dad's throat.

'Do you see anything?' he asked.

'No, I don't see a thing,' said Mom. 'Don't you feel well?' she asked.

'I think I'm coming down with something,' said Dad.

'Maybe I'll call work and tell them I'm not coming in tomorrow?'

'Dad,' I said. 'If Uncle Leo still had the miraculous medicine, you would never be sick. You could go to work every day.'

'Miraculous medicine?' said Dad.

'Yes. It's a medicine that cures all the illnesses in the world,' I explained. 'But Uncle Leo didn't manage to get it.'

'Good thing,' said Mom, 'because I think Dad wants to lie on the couch tomorrow and watch TV too.'

Uncle Leo in Chocolateland

The following Wednesday, Graham and I were both back on our feet. We were sitting in the kitchen, eating chocolate cake with chocolate syrup. I looked at Graham's piece of cake. It looked bigger than mine.

'Mom!' I said. 'Why did Graham get a bigger piece?'

Mom looked at my piece and then looked at Graham's, but Graham had quickly taken a giant bite out of his piece.

'I don't see any difference,' said Mom. 'They're roughly the same size.'

Graham smiled. He was happy. I looked at Phoebe. She was still a baby. She couldn't get a piece of cake like me and Graham.

'Mom,' I said. 'Don't you always say that we have to learn to share equally?'

'Yes,' said Mom.

'That means that Phoebe should get a piece of cake, too, doesn't it?'

'Yes,' said Mom.

'So maybe I can have her piece? She won't eat it anyway, since she's a baby.'

'Phoebe will get all the pieces she deserves when she's the right age. And besides, you two have already had enough sweets for today,' said Mom, going off with Phoebe to change her diaper.

Graham and I were left in the kitchen. We looked at the rest of the chocolate cake sitting on the table.

Graham picked up the knife to cut another piece of cake.

'Graham!' I said. 'Mom said we shouldn't eat any more.'

Graham stopped and thought for a moment. 'We'll share a piece,' he said. 'Should I cut it in half?'

But just as Graham started cutting the cake, someone walked into the kitchen. Graham was startled and dropped the knife. It was Uncle Leo.

'Andy was about to eat more cake,' said Graham.

'I was not!' I said. '*You* were about to cut a slice!'

Uncle Leo said nothing and sat down with us. He looked at the chocolate cake with a smile and said, 'Chocolate, chocolate, chocolate...I do so love chocolate.'

'Do you want a piece?' I asked.

'Certainly,' said Uncle Leo.

I cut a slice for Uncle Leo, but Graham and I didn't take any more.

Uncle Leo took a bite and said, with his mouth full of cake, 'We are so lucky.'

'Why are we lucky?' asked Graham.

'We're lucky we can eat chocolate,' said Uncle Leo.

Graham and I looked at Uncle Leo, but we didn't understand what he was talking about.

'There are places where it's dangerous to eat chocolate,' he said.

'Dangerous to eat chocolate?' I said, surprised. 'Where?'

'I'll tell you about it,' said Uncle Leo. 'I once went hiking in the Swiss desert. I took supplies with me for the way: a map, walking shoes, a hat, a canteen and pickles, in case I got hungry. I walked and walked, and really enjoyed the trip. But when I wanted to return home, I couldn't. I checked the map but I couldn't understand where I was. I had lost my way. I walked and walked and walked some more. Eventually, I ran out of water and got very thirsty. My throat was dry. My head ached. I wanted a drink very badly, but my canteen was completely empty. I didn't know what to do. If I didn't drink soon, I would die of thirst. People can't live without water! I continued walking, hoping I would find a solution.

'Suddenly, I saw a lone faucet in the middle of the desert. *Impossible,* I thought. *How can there be a faucet in the middle of the desert. I must be imagining it.* But I was so thirsty that I went up to the faucet anyway and turned the handle. I turned it and got quite a surprise!

I was shocked, in fact! Water didn't come out of that faucet,' said Uncle Leo, looking at us.

'Was the water shut off?' I asked.

'No, not at all,' said Uncle Leo. 'Hot chocolate came out of the faucet! I bent over and drank. It was the best hot chocolate I had ever tasted.

It was just sweet enough and just warm and thick enough. I had never tasted such wonderful hot chocolate!' said Uncle Leo. Now he closed his eyes and breathed heavily.

'Uncle Leo, how could there have been a hot chocolate faucet in the middle of the desert?' asked Graham.

'Exactly!' said Uncle Leo. 'I was amazed too. How could there be a hot chocolate faucet in the middle of the desert? But just then I smelled something I will never forget. I smelled a marvellously sweet aroma, the aroma of chocolate. I raised my head, looked at the horizon, and saw something strange and surprising. Far off on the horizon stood a big chocolate cake—an enormous chocolate cake. It was brown and shining.

'As soon as I saw the cake, I couldn't stop. I left behind the pickles, the hat and the map. I put one pickle in my pocket, just in case I got hungry, and quickly set off towards the chocolate cake. I couldn't stop walking. My feet carried me toward the cake.

I made good progress and soon saw that in the middle of the chocolate cake towered a mountain of whipped cream topped with a red cherry.

"'Oh my! I must have a bite of that cake!" I told myself. "I must lick that whipped cream! I must taste that cherry!" I continued walking until I reached the cake. It was humongous. I climbed up the cake. I kept telling myself, "Before I eat the cake, I must taste that whipped cream." I marched as if in a trance towards the whipped cream mountain. When I reached it, I debated with myself about what I should do first. *Should I lick the whipped cream first and then eat the cherry, or would it be better to climb the mountain of whipped cream, eat the cherry, and then lick the whipped cream?* I thought about it and, in the end, decided to taste the whipped cream first. I stuck my finger out towards the whipped cream, but just then I heard a shout, "Hey! What do you think you're doing?"

'I tried to figure out where the voice was coming from. I looked around me. Everything was chocolate-coloured. I didn't see anybody. I stuck my finger out

towards the whipped cream once again, but before I could touch it, I heard the same voice again, "You're so insolent! Don't you dare touch the mountain!"

'I couldn't understand who was yelling at me. I couldn't understand where the voice was coming from. I looked around me, and suddenly saw a chocolate man standing on the chocolate cake. It was hard to see him because he was brown, just like the chocolate all around him.

'The man came up to me and roared, "How dare you approach our holy mountain? How dare you touch our holy mountain?"

'"I just want to taste this whipped cream," I said. "It looks fantastic."

'"Taste the holy mountain? *Our* holy mountain? No one touches or tastes it!"

'"Well then," I asked. "Can I just eat the cherry on top?"

'"I can't believe this! Eat our God?"

'"Your God?" I asked.

'"Yes, our God," said the chocolate man. "Our God sits high on the mountaintop, and every morning we pray to him, begging, 'Give us a sweet life!' And every evening we pray to him, saying, 'Thank you for such a sweet life!' And now you plan to eat our God? I'll take you to our king's palace and have you put on trial!" he said, grabbing my shoulders.

"'I'm sorry, I'm sorry, I didn't know," I cried. "I thought this was whipped cream that could be eaten. I thought I could take a bite of the cherry. Please, let me go. I didn't know this mountain was sacred!"

'I tried to escape, but then more chocolate people showed up and surrounded me. Some were made of bittersweet chocolate, some of milk chocolate, and others of white chocolate. They all held me. They picked me up and carried me to the palace so I could be put on trial.'

'What did you do?' asked Graham. 'Did you manage to get away from them?'

'I tried, Graham, I really tried. I looked at the chocolate people and even thought of taking a bite out of them. They looked super tasty. Everything around me looked delicious, and I could barely control myself. But the chocolate people had tied my hands and feet with special chocolate ropes.

'We reached the palace. It was no ordinary palace.

The entire palace was made of countless kinds of chocolate. The walls, the spires, the door frames, the stairs, even the flags—everything was made of chocolate.

'They took me to the chocolate king. He looked at me severely and asked, "Who are you?"

"'I'm Uncle Leo," I replied.

"'You were planning to eat the holy whipped cream mountain? What a disgrace! What blasphemy! What do you have to say in your defence?"

"'I didn't know that the mountain and the cherry were sacred, Your Majesty. Where I come from, people eat whipped cream and cherries, and chocolate too."

"'Good Cherries!" cried the king's ministers. "This is unheard of! He is a dangerous enemy! He wants to destroy us all!"

"'Tie him to the pillar!" ordered the king, and two soldiers tied me to a pillar next to the king's table, using ultra-strong chocolate ropes.

'I stood there, all tied up, and didn't know what to do. I tried to break free of the ropes, but they were too strong. How could I get away? How could I explain to the king and his people that I had no intention of hurting them?

'While I was standing there, tied in ropes, the king was served a meal. He ate chocolate chicken and chocolate rice, and drank a chocolate drink. All the courses were made of chocolate. At the end of the meal, a servant offered the king a box of candy for dessert. I was curious to see what the king would have for dessert. If all the courses in the meal were made of chocolate, what would the dessert be made of? When the box was opened and I saw the dessert, I was shocked. I was appalled!'

Now, in the kitchen, Uncle Leo stopped talking. He balled his hands into fists and gave us a shaken look.

'Uncle Leo,' I said, 'what was in the box of candy?'

'Fingers,' said Uncle Leo. 'The box had human fingers in it. The king ate real fingers for dessert. After he finished eating them, he looked at me and said, "Tomorrow we'll make dessert out of *your* fingers!"

'"Out of my fingers?" I asked fearfully.

'"Yes," said the king. "A royal dessert." And he left the room.

'All night long I thought about what to do. I didn't know how I could convince the king not to make dessert out of my fingers. I thought about all the wonderful things that I do with my fingers, and I really didn't want to part with them. I really didn't want my fingers to be turned into the royal dessert.

'In the morning, the king ordered that I be released from the ropes. He sat on his throne and commanded, "Bring the royal knife!"

'A servant came in carrying a chocolate knife on a pillow.

'"Test the royal knife!" ordered the king.

'Another servant laid a large, hard chunk of chocolate in the middle of the hall. A third servant picked up the knife, raised it in the air, and cut the chocolate with one blow. I knew that in another minute my fingers would also meet this fate. I trembled in fear. The king commanded, "Prepare for me the royal dessert!"

'I was taken to the middle of the room. They laid the palm of my hand on the table. A servant swung the knife above my fingers. At the last moment, I remembered something. I remembered that I had one sour pickle in my pocket. "Wait!" I called out. "Wait a minute! Just a second! I have a special suggestion!"

'The servant stopped and placed the knife on the table. The king looked at me curiously.

"'Your Majesty, I would like you to taste something," I said.

"'Taste something? What should I be tasting besides your fingers?"

"'I want you to taste something much better than my fingers."

"'Better than your fingers?" wondered the king. "What could be better than the royal dessert?"

'I took the pickle out of my pocket and handed it to the king. The king looked at the pickle suspiciously.

"'What is it?" he asked. "What is this thing?"

"'It's a sour pickle," I said.

"'Sowprickle? What is sow?"

"'Sour pickle. Sour is a special taste, different from sweet," I explained to the king.

"'And you eat it?" asked the king.

"'Yes, I eat it every day. I love sour pickles. Taste it, give it a try. If you don't like it, you can spit it out," I said.

'The king hesitated for a moment and thought about it, then he opened his mouth and took a bite of the sour pickle. I didn't know what he would say. I didn't know if he would like the taste or hate it. After all, this was the first time he had ever tasted anything sour.

'The king thought for a moment, took another bite of the pickle, raised his eyebrows and then smiled. He said, "The taste of heaven! It tastes wonderful! It tastes excellent! I have never tasted anything this good! Words cannot express how good this is. Tell me, do you have another one of these sowprickles?"

'"Yes, yes," I told the king happily. "Sour pickles. If you set me free, I can bring you a whole jar of sour pickles."

'And so the king announced, "I hereby command that Uncle Leo be set free and that he give me a jar of sowprickles. From this day forward, a slice of sowprickle will be the royal dessert that I eat after every sweet meal. I wish to thank Uncle Leo for introducing me to new tastes, and for adding some sowness to my sweet life. Thank you, Uncle Leo."

'"My pleasure, Your Highness," I said. "When life is too sweet, a little sourness is good for the soul."

'And indeed, I walked with the king's servants to the hot chocolate faucet, where I had left the jar of pickles, and the servants even pointed out the way for me to get back home.'

'A sour pickle for dessert...' said Graham, and we both laughed.

'Lucky they didn't cut off your fingers,' I said.

'Really lucky,' said Uncle Leo. 'But that's nothing compared to the time someone wanted to fry me like a schnitzel.'

'Like a schnitzel? Who wanted to fry you?' Graham and I asked.

'I'll tell you about it next Wednesday,' said Uncle Leo.

After dinner, I said, 'Mom, can I please have some more chocolate cake?'

'Yes, it's really good cake,' added Graham. 'Can we?'

Mom thought for a moment and then said, 'All right. Would you like some too?' she asked Dad.

'Uh…no, no, give it to the kids,' he said.

Mom handed Phoebe to Dad and went to the cake pan. I hoped that this time I would get a bigger piece than Graham. But when Mom looked in the pan, she only found crumbs.

'What's this?' Mom said. 'Where did the cake go?'

'Andy! You ate all the cake! Admit that you ate it!' shouted Graham.

'I didn't touch the cake!' I shouted back.

I glared at Graham, and Graham glared at me. Mom glared at both of us. Phoebe smiled at Mom.

Dad was the only one who didn't look at any of us.

'So,' Mom said. 'Who ate it?'

'Um…' said Dad. 'I…thought…I mean, I was hungry and…there wasn't much cake left, so I ate it. It came out really well. You make amazing cakes.'

'Dad, you're like Uncle Leo in the land of chocolate,' I said. 'After so much chocolate, in the end, you'll be begging to eat a sour pickle.'

'A sour pickle?' asked Dad, astonished.

'Yes,' I said. 'When life is too sweet, a little sourness is good for the soul.'

Uncle Leo, a Living Doll

All week long, we waited for Uncle Leo to visit us again. On Wednesday, Graham and I were already sitting in the balcony when Uncle Leo came in. Graham immediately jumped up and asked him. 'Uncle Leo, why did someone want to fry you like a schnitzel?'

Uncle Leo sat down and started telling us. 'Once, I went for a trip to the land of monsters in the Swiss desert. I had never met a them before, and I was curious. I wanted to see monsters. I searched for many days in the mountains and valleys, but I didn't come across a single monster. I got very tired. I had to rest. I decided to sleep for a while in the shade of a tree. I lay down and soon fell asleep. I don't know how long I slept, but I opened my eyes when

I heard someone saying:

'"Look what I found!"

'When I opened my eyes, I saw an old lady monster leaning over me. She was very big. Her face was scary and her teeth were sharp. I was so frightened that I didn't move and I didn't say a word. The monstress called out to her husband, and he came and looked at me from above. The husband monster's face was scary too. I was so terrified that I couldn't move.

'"He just opened his eyes!" cried the monstress.

'The old monster looked and me and said, "How lucky! You've found a human! That's great!"

'I was happy to see that the old monster was excited, but I quickly understood that his reason for being happy was very bad for me, and that I'd better not move.'

'Why, Uncle Leo?' asked Graham. 'Why was it better for you to not move?'

'Because the old lady monstress said, "This is great! I'll cook this human into a wonderful soup. I'll add carrots and a few roots, and maybe even some noodles."

'"My dear wife," said the husband monster. "You know how much I love your human-being soup, but maybe you should use him to make schnitzel?"

'I heard what the monster couple was saying, so I didn't move and I didn't make a sound. Finally the husband monster said, "Hold on a second, something's funny here. Something's not right. Have you noticed he's not moving? Have you noticed he isn't speaking? Humans usually move and talk. I'm not sure this is really a human being." The monster poked me, but I didn't move. I froze in place like a statue.

"'You're right," said the monstress. "And as far as I know, humans have a lot of hair on their heads. This thing only has four hairs."

"'This is weird," said the monster. "Really weird." And he sank into silent thought. "He smells yummy like a human. And look, he's wearing glasses. Only humans wear glasses."

"'But, my dear husband," said the monstress. "Humans move. This thing doesn't move. Humans talk. This thing doesn't talk. This looks like a human, it's true, but I really don't think it is!"

"'So maybe this is a doll that looks just like a human," said the monster.

'The monstress thought for a moment and then said, "You're right. This must be a human doll."

"'I've got an idea!" said the monster. "We'll send this doll to Gimme!"

"'What a marvellous idea!" said the monstress. "She's got a birthday coming up. She's so sweet! Our adorable granddaughter is just going to love this doll."

The monstress picked me up like a toy and they took me to the local post office. I didn't move a muscle the whole way there. At the post office, they put me into a box and closed me up inside it. They put a stamp on the box and sent me to their granddaughter Gimme for her birthday.'

Uncle Leo fell silent. He took his handkerchief out of his pocket and wiped his glasses with it.

'But, Uncle Leo,' I said. 'What did you do inside the box?'

'It was dark inside the box, and there was barely any air,' Uncle Leo went on. 'I had trouble breathing. It was very stuffy inside the box. I didn't know how much time had passed, but finally I heard a voice talking outside the box:

"'Mommy! Daddy! Grandma and Grandpa sent me a birthday present!

Yippee!" It was Gimme.

'Gimme's parents opened the box. As before, I didn't move and I didn't make a sound.

'The mother monster said, "Grandma and Grandpa sent you a human being! I'll cook him into a wonderful soup, and I'll add carrots and a few roots, and maybe even some noodles."

'I was sure they were going to cook me right away, but then the father monster said, "He's not a real human being. He's a human doll. Don't you see? He doesn't move and he doesn't talk. Gimme, Grandma and Grandpa sent you a new toy."

'I sighed in relief. Both Gimme and her parents thought I was a human doll.

'That was how I became Gimme's toy. She loved playing with me. She dressed me in new clothes. She put me in her dollhouse. She sang songs to me and even pretended to give me a bath. Gimme loved me so much, she wouldn't let anyone else play with me. "He's mine!" she screamed at anyone who came near me. "Don't touch him! He's mine and only mine!"'

'But, Uncle Leo,' said

Graham, 'if you moved, they would find out you're a real human and they would cook you!'

'That's right. I didn't move even a little bit. I knew that I had to act like a doll so they wouldn't discover that I was a living human being! It was very difficult. Every time Gimme turned around and wasn't looking my way, I moved a bit. I scratched my head. I moved my arms or wiggled my toes. When they called Gimme to eat lunch and she left me alone in her room, I could move around, stretch, go to the bathroom. I would sneak outside and eat from the giant raspberry bush in the garden. But as soon as I heard Gimme coming back to her room, I would return to the same position I had been in before, and not move. It was really hard.

'Time passed, and eventually Gimme wasn't excited about me any more. She got tired of playing with me. She left me on a shelf next to the other toys and started playing other games. I sat on the shelf, and whenever Gimme was in the room, I didn't move and didn't make a sound. I wanted to escape, but I couldn't. Every time I tried to get away, I almost got caught and had to return to the shelf and not move.

'But one day, something horrible happened! Gimme was playing with a toy elephant that was missing its head. She told the toy elephant, "It's such a shame you don't have a head. Maybe I can get a head for you?" She approached

the shelf I was sitting on and surveyed the toys. She looked at me, lifted me up, and said to the elephant, "Maybe I'll take the head off of this doll and put it on you. Yes, that's what I'll do. I'll take its head off."

'When I heard what Gimme said, I panicked. Gimme was planning to fasten my head on the elephant doll! She was planning to take off my head because she thought I was just an old toy. But I wasn't a toy! And my head was attached to my body! It couldn't just be removed!

'Gimme took me down from the shelf and grabbed my head. I did my best not to shake, but when Gimme started pulling on my head, I cried out, "No! Don't take my

head off! I'm not a toy! You can't just pull my head off!"

'Gimme looked at me in shock. She was astounded. All this time, she had thought that I was just a human doll, and now she realized I was a real human being.

"'Gimme," I immediately said. "I am not a doll. If you take my head off, I will die. Please don't do it!"

"'Mommy! Daddy!" shouted Gimme.

"'Gimme, Gimme," I begged. "Please don't tell anyone that I'm not a doll!" I didn't want to be cooked.

'But Gimme kept calling anyway, "Mommy! Daddy! Come quick!"

'Gimme's mother and father ran into the room.

"'Mommy, Daddy, he's not really a doll. He's a real human," Gimme told them.

"'Are you sure?" asked Gimme's mother.

"'I'm sure," said Gimme.

'Gimme's mother and father looked at me. I was shaking with fear. They saw that I wasn't a doll. They saw that I was a live human.

'Gimme's mother said, "A real human? That's great! Excellent! I'll cook him into a wonderful soup. I'll put him in boiling water, and I'll add onion, and I'll add carrots and a few roots, and maybe even some noodles. What do you say?" the mother monster asked her daughter and husband.

"'Maybe a schnitzel would be better?" said Gimme's father. "Of course, I love your soups, my dear wife, but..."

"'No! Don't touch him! He's mine and only mine!" screamed Gimme.

"'But my dear monsterette, he's a real human being. Don't you want me to make him into a schnitzel for you? You love schnitzel, don't you?"

'Gimme thought for a moment and then thought some more, and then she said, "All right, yes, I do. I want a schnitzel!"

"'We'll make it together!" said the mother monster.

"'Yay!" cried Gimme.

"'Please! Listen to me!" I cried. "Please don't make me into a schnitzel or a soup!" But the monster family didn't listen to me. The father monster picked me up, took me to the kitchen and put me in a cage. Gimme sat down at the table and waited for her schnitzel. The mother monster poured breadcrumbs into a large bowl. The father monster placed a frying pan on the stove, poured oil into it and lit the flame. The oil started heating up. I didn't know what to do. In another minute,

I would be covered with breadcrumbs, fried in a pan, and turned into a schnitzel!'

Uncle Leo looked at us silently. He folded his handkerchief and put it back in his pocket.

'Uncle Leo,' said Graham worriedly, 'they didn't fry you, did they?'

'The oil in the frying pan was boiling hot and bubbling,' continued Uncle Leo. 'I didn't know what to do. Suddenly an idea came to me. I whispered to Gimme, "Gimme, come here a second. Come over here. I want to tell you something."

'Gimme came closer to the cage. "What do you want to tell me?" she asked.

'"Stories," I said. "I'll tell you about my adventures until lunch is ready." And indeed I did.'

'What did you tell her?' I asked.

'I told her about how I became the most famous man in the kingdom of Nullistan. I told her how I almost got the medicine that would cure all the diseases in the world. I told her about the whipped cream mountain in Chocolateland. Gimme listened to my stories. She enjoyed them. Then she looked at the frying pan and the boiling hot oil, and said, "You're cute. You tell fascinating stories. It would be a shame to make you into a schnitzel. I'm going to set you free."

'Gimme opened the cage, put me in a shoebox and took me outside to a field, without her mother and father noticing. She set me free in the field. I walked among the weeds and waved goodbye to Gimme. All of the sudden she called out, "Uncle Leo, wait!"

'I was frightened, because I thought Gimme might have changed her mind and decided that she'd rather eat a human schnitzel after all. But Gimme smiled at me. She untied the kerchief from around her neck and gave it to me.

'"This kerchief will be a souvenir of me for you," she said.

'"Thank you, Gimme, I will always treasure it," I said and walked away.

'And I really did keep Gimme's kerchief,' said Uncle Leo. 'And I've brought it for you.'

'Really?' I said.

Uncle Leo took a giant handkerchief out of a bag. It was so big that it covered the whole table.

After Uncle Leo had left, Mom and Dad came out to the balcony with our sister Phoebe. Mom said, 'It's so good to see you two not fighting.' And then she noticed Gimme's handkerchief. 'Where did that tablecloth come from?' she asked. 'It looks familiar.'

'No, Mom,' I said. 'It's not a tablecloth. It's a kerchief that Uncle Leo got from a giant little girl monster. Her name was Gimme.'

'Yes,' said Graham, 'in the Swiss desert. The monsters wanted to make him into a schnitzel, but in the end their daughter let him go. Then she gave him her kerchief as a memento.'

Mom and Dad looked curiously at the big kerchief covering the table.

'Well,' said Mom, 'we really did need a tablecloth.'

'So let's eat our dinner on Gimme's kerchief,' I suggested.

'That's an excellent idea,' said Mom, and we all went to make food together.

Uncle Leo keeps visiting us every Wednesday and tells us about his fascinating adventures all around the world. It's fun. And Mom and Dad? They still remind us ever so often not to fight and not to eat too much chocolate and not to watch television all day long. And maybe that makes sense, because otherwise we wouldn't have time for anything else.